I CHOOSE YOU

Written by Patricia Lei Murray

Illustrated by Stephanie Britt

ISLAND HERITAGE™
PUBLISHING
A DIVISION OF THE MADDEN CORPORATION

Published and distributed by

ISLAND HERITAGE™
P U B L I S H I N G
A DIVISION OF THE MADDEN CORPORATION

94-411 Kō'aki Street, Waipahu, Hawai'i 96797-2806
Orders: (800) 468-2800 • Information: (808) 564-8800
Fax: (808) 564-8877
islandheritage.com

Written by Patricia Lei Murray
Illustrated by Stephanie Britt

ISBN: 1-59700-929-6
First Edition, First Printing—2010
SFO 100809

I dedicate this book to my Aunty La'ikealoha, which means "peaceful love". She was the inspiration for this book, as well as all the "Aunties" who make a loving difference daily in the lives of children everywhere.

~ Patricia Lei Murray

Chapter 1

IT'S TIME

The big people were talking in the kitchen, and I was listening because I thought I heard them say "La'i," and that's my name.

It was Saturday, Chinatown day for Aunty Ku'ulei. After she finished shopping, she always stopped to visit. She brought bunches of heliconia and fresh ginger from her yard, Hawaiian food, like fish and *poi*, *poke* with *limu kohu* and *'inamona*, and even Chinese food, *look funn* and *manapua*.

Oh, the kitchen smelled so good! But, you couldn't just barge in there. You had to hang around outside the door until you heard them call, "OK, you guys, come eat!" Then, not just one, but all four of us girls would come out of nowhere. There were many hugs and kisses for Aunty, and over the noise you could hear Tūtū say, "Here, go, take that outside...and eat nice, don't make a mess."

I heard Aunty Kuʻu say she was going on another trip. Every time she went, she took one of us with her. I hadn't had my turn yet. Could this be it?

Aunty Kuʻu had no children, but she treated us all like her very own. She was always doing something special. One time, she went to Molokaʻi to sing and took Kanani. Another time, when she went to Maui to show the ladies how to weave *lau hala* baskets, she took Kalamau. Once she went to Waimea on the Big

Island to show the ladies how to make fancy quilts, and she took Pikake.

I remember my sisters telling me when it was their turn to go with her and they got on the plane, no matter which one she took, she would hug them close and say just like a secret, "I choose you, Bebe, because you the *pretty* one, just like Aunty!" And together they would LAUGH, and they all just loved it. Oh, it *had* to be my turn!

After my sisters went out, I stayed in the back bedroom by the kitchen door slowly eating my manapua. I heard my mother say, "Oh, wow! So far! What you have to do over there?"

"Well," said Aunty Ku'u, "I have some business with Aunty Kilohana and her *hula hālau*, school, and since La'i is our dancer, I wanted to take her with me. What you think?"

I choked on my manapua. *What you think???* Ask me what I think!

"Paris!" Tūtū's voice rose. "They have hula hālau over there?"

Paris!!! I squealed and quickly clapped both hands over my mouth.

"Yes, and they want to come to Hawaiʻi to perform in the World International Hula Exposition. I'll do whatever I can to help them," Aunty Kuʻu said.

Just then Mommy called, "Laʻi—kealoha!"

Oh, Oh, my name again! It's time.

In an instant, I was in the kitchen doorway. I couldn't help smiling as I asked in my sweetest voice, "You calling me?"

"Oh, we knew you were there the whole time," Tūtū smiled. "*Noho ma‘a ne‘i*," sit here.

Mommy spoke and Daddy looked on, smiling. "School is finishing and summer break will soon be here. Daddy and I notice that you have been working hard to keep your grades up, and that's good. Aunty Ku‘ulei has asked if she can take you with her to a very exciting place. Nobody in our family has gone to such a far place. She is going to Paris, France. Do you know where that is?"

"Oh, Yes," I said loudly, "we talk about..."

"Let's look it up," interrupted Aunty Ku‘u. She whipped out the folded world map and spread it on the table for everyone to see.

"Oh, please can I—may I go?" I pleaded. "We talk about France in school. I haven't gone with Aunty yet. It's my turn. Oh, please, please! I really want to go."

"La'i, look like you win the big prize!" Daddy laughed.

I ran outside yelling and jumping up and down. The other girls were riding the swings in the big mango tree. When I told them about Paris, they all screamed in disbelief, "WHAT! NOT! WHO SAID?"

Chapter 2

IT HAPPENED!

Aunty Kuʻu said we would leave in a month, so we had lots to do. She invited me to her house, and we sat together and talked about all the important papers we had to get, like pictures, passports, and visas. It all sounded so important—and so exciting!

Finally came the day we were going to leave. The whole family gathered to say goodbye. Aunty Kuʻu counted all the bags and tied big strips of bright Hawaiian fabric to the handles so we could tell right away which bags were ours. She even made sure the special boxes of ferns for Aunty Kilohana were marked well. She checked that I had my belly pack, and that my ID, passport, and money were safe. She wore a quilted jacket with many hidden pockets. Even her purse had hidden pockets.

Tūtū led us in *pule*, prayer, to keep us safe. I kissed my sisters, Mommy, Daddy, and Tūtū goodbye many times. Of course, they all said, "Listen to Aunty and don't get lost."

Daddy held out his hand and said, "Here, keep this money safe and close. We've been saving it for you."

I looked at it and tears filled my eyes. I knew they didn't have much money to go around, but they had saved this money for me. I vowed to buy something special for them.

Aunty Ku'u got in the front of the car with Daddy, and I squeezed in the back with all the bags. As we drove away, I looked through the rear window and saw our ʻohana, family, all lined up on the road waving and jumping up and down. Tears came again and dripped down into my sweet plumeria lei.

We got to the airport, and Aunty crossed her fingers that our bags were not overweight. When the airline people handed us our boarding cards, she breathed out a big "All Right!" and we were on our way.

We waited in the boarding area until our rows were called, then we picked up our stuff and stood in line. My heart was pounding. I looked up at Aunty, and she seemed to know how I was feeling, because she hugged me. In no time, we found our seats. Aunty gave me the window. I looked out and saw our bags on the belt moving slowly into the belly of the plane.

As soon as the plane took off, Aunty Kuʻulei pulled me close to her and with a big smile, she whispered a secret, "Laʻi, you know what? Aunty choose *you* to come with me...because...you the *pretty* one, just like Aunty!" We LAUGHED and I turned and hugged her tight. I had been waiting all this time just to hear her say that very thing to me.

It was late, and we were tired, so it wasn't long before we were both asleep. When we opened our eyes, the sun was a big red ball sitting in the clouds like a cherry on a cake. Something smelled really good. I looked down the aisle and saw the attendant handing out big, warm, chocolate chip macadamia nut cookies with milk. *This must be heaven!* I thought.

After stopovers in California and New York, we were finally on our way to France. The attendants spoke French, and it wasn't easy to know what they were saying. But I sure knew what was happening when the food came! It was fancy and delicious, especially the chocolate dessert.

When dinner was over, we could hardly keep our eyes open. Aunty said that traveling this far could be very tiring. We said our little pule holding hands, got comfortable in our blankets and said, "Goodnight world!"

Chapter 3

THE CITY OF LIGHTS

When I woke up, I heard Aunty say, "There she is, La'i!"

I looked out the window and all I could do, was to breathe in,"Ahhhhhh," and breathe out, "Looook!" At least a million little lights sparkled back at me as we floated over Paris, the City of Lights.

We went through customs with all our papers, and who was there to greet us as we came through the doors? Aunty Kilohana! "*Bonsoir, ma chère Ku'ulei*," Greetings, my dear Ku'ulei, "*et Bonsoir, ma petite fleur,* La'i," and greetings my little flower, La'i, she called. She gently kissed us on both cheeks and handed each of us a little bouquet of fresh flowers. I was so happy to meet her and finally be in France!

Our suitcases fit just right in the back of the van next to the big *ipu heke*, drum, and the long *kāla'au*, sticks. Stuffed in the corner was a tall sack with skinny breads sticking out.

"Aunty, what's this?" I asked, pointing to the bread.

"Oh, that is our *baguette* to have with some nice *chocolat chaud*, hot chocolate, when we get home. Then you can sleep."

That sounded like a good idea to me. The two aunties talked and laughed up front as the van bumped away from the airport. I found two aloha print pillows in the back and a blanket. My eyes were so heavy. I just closed them for a minute, and before I knew it, I was fast asleep.

When I woke up, we were in the city, driving through small streets with tall old buildings on both sides. The lampposts were lit and you could see flowers growing over fancy black window railings. We swerved into a busy street with lots of traffic.

"Aunty, what's that in the middle of the road with all the cars going around?" I asked.

"That's *l'Arc de Triomphe*," said Aunty Kilohana, "and we're driving on the *Avenue des Champs-Élysées* that leads to it. People can go to the top of the arch and see the whole city laid out like a big star! One day we will go, but right now, we're going home."

Leilani, Aunty Kilohana's daughter, met us at the door and took us right into the kitchen. The chocolat chaud was so *'ono* with the crusty bread and real butter. The kitchen was warm and cozy. They even let me dunk my bread in the cocoa.

Aunty Kilohana led Aunty Ku'u and I down the hall to a blue bedroom with floating white lace curtains and a big bed with fluffy white pillows. She showed us our own bathroom that had a big old tub with what looked like duck feet on the bottom. I could hardly wait to get inside! I liked the fancy wallpaper and even the blue and white flowers on the toilet paper.

"*Mahalo nui loa, Kilohana,*" Thank you, Kilohana, said Aunty Ku'u. We both hugged her. "*Je vous en prie,*" It is my pleasure. She hugged us back. "*Bonne nuit, mes chéries,*" Good night, my dear ones.

We felt at home even though we knew we were far away. After our baths we said a pule and lay awake quietly talking about all the things we had done. I went to sleep smiling, holding Aunty Ku'u's hand, and once again picturing the lights of Paris in my mind.

Chapter 4

OUT AND ABOUT

Morning came with the clanking sounds of garbage trucks, but good smells came from the kitchen. We washed up, made our bed, and went off to find Aunty Kilohana. As we went down the hall, we met Leilani and Lala, her fluffy little dog.

"*Bonjour*," said Leilani, hugging us. She led us to the kitchen where Aunty Kilohana was ready with breakfast.

"*Bonjour, comment ça va?*" Good morning, how are you, she asked. We all replied, "*Ça va, ça va bien, merci,*" We're fine, we're good, thank you.

For breakfast, there was a pretty basket of yummy French pastries to choose from. My mouth watered as Aunty Kilohana pointed out the *croissants, pain au chocolat*, chocolate-filled croissants, and *pain au raison*, raisin-filled croissants, and more chocolat chaud and orange juice.

On our first day in Paris, we went on errands with Aunty Kilohana, chugging down the streets along the famous Seine River. There was so much more to see during the day—people everywhere, strolling, sitting on benches, meeting at outside cafés, taking pictures, pedaling bicycles, riding on buses with seats on the roof. Summertime was a popular time to visit Paris, but I just couldn't believe that WE were here, too.

Soon we were going over a bridge, and there right before my eyes, I saw what looked like the biggest church in the world. Aunty Kuʻu said it was called the *Cathedral de Notre Dame.*

"You must see it from the inside," she said.

We walked through the cathedral's heavy brown doors with lots of other people and stood in the quiet. We moved toward the front and saw all the beautiful stained glass windows. Aunty Kilohana said that the colorful windows were used to tell Bible stories. They stretched high into the ceiling as if they were reaching to touch heaven. We sat for a while and listened to the organ play. I thought about Tūtū and how she would have loved to see this place.

After our visit to Notre Dame we took our picnic basket to a little park close by. We watched a little band of French musicians play on the bridge and saw people sailing down the Seine on *bateaux mouches*, French riverboats.

On our way back home, Aunty Kilohana took us past the famous flower markets along the river. People were carrying armfuls of flowers. Even Aunty Ku'u bought some for the house.

By the time we had had our dinner and crawled into bed, it was raining outside, a little *kilihune* rain, a soft misty rain.

Chapter 5

HULA SISTERS ABROAD

Next morning, my eyes flew open when I heard a crash of bottles on the street. *What is that? Garbage trucks again? Oh, well, time to get up*, I told myself. *This is a big day. Up, up, up!*

It was hula day. Aunty Kilohana was taking us to *Hālau Hula o Mānoa* in Paris to meet students my own age.

As we drove through the city, I got a little nervous thinking about the girls I was going to meet. *Would they like me?*

We turned down a little street, and I saw some girls waiting on the sidewalk while others were being dropped off. They all had bags with their hula instruments inside, and they were wearing their *pāʻū* skirts, just like the one I had. We went up the winding staircase and through the doors, and we heard giggling, laughing, and speaking in French while the girls found places to put their things.

Aunty Kilohana called the class to order in Hawaiian. And they understood! The room quieted and she gently began, "*Mākaukau?* Ready? *Ae*, yes," they answered. Then I couldn't believe my ears. After all that French, there was clear, Hawaiian chanting. It was Aunty Nona's famous *Oli Aloha*, Chant of Welcome. Aunty Kilohana introduced Aunty Kuʻu and me to the girls and told them where we were from and a little about us. She even invited me, when I was ready, to dance with the girls. Their smiles made me feel welcome, but for the time being, I just wanted to watch.

They began their hula by practicing all the basic steps to the beat of the *ipu*, then a few other chants they were learning. To my surprise, they started to do *Lili'u E*, a chant I knew, and the motions were the same! After a while, Aunty Kilohana looked over to me and, with a smile and a wave of her hand, she invited me to dance.

Somehow, I wasn't scared. I was about to do something I loved. My dancing feet lifted me up and took me into the line with my new awaiting friends. I felt at home. I danced right along with them, moving and turning together like we had done this many times before. It felt so good not to be scared.

At the break, the girls came up to say hello. They wanted to know all about Hawai'i, the sunshine, and if the ocean was really that blue! They even asked me to dance with them at the Bastille Dance Festival the next week.

"I'm not sure I could do that," I said, blinking.

"Oh, sure you can!" they answered. During dinner, as we discussed the Festival, the Aunties looked over at me and explained that there was a costume for me, if I would like to participate.

"Really? May I—just one song? Is that OK?"

"Of course it's OK!" the aunties laughed, "We were hoping you would say that."

Before we went to sleep, Aunty Ku'u and I talked again about our day. I rolled toward her and said, "Aunty, I really loved hearing the girls chant in Hawaiian, and they're not even

Hawaiian, they're French! Aunty Kilohana and Leilani are good teachers, aren't they?"

"Yes, they are," said Aunty Ku'u. "That's how important things are handed down to other generations, La'i. When we share what is precious to us, we keep it alive, it is who we are, and we live on."

She kissed my hands and whispered, "*Bonne nuit, ma coeur*," Good night, my sweetheart.

Chapter 6

PRINCESS FOR A DAY

The next few days went by swiftly. Aunty Ku'u and I were on our own because Aunty Kilohana was away. We visited the Eiffel Tower and rode the high elevators to the very top. The wind was blowing so hard I thought I would fly away as I looked at the city below. We could see l'Arc de Triomphe standing right in the middle of the road with all the cars going around like little ants in a race.

One day, Aunty Ku'u received a call from Aunty Becca and Uncle Scott who were back in Paris for the summer. We are not really related, but we love each other just like family. They wanted to know if they could take us to see *Le Chateau Vaux-le-Vicomte*, a beautiful castle outside Paris.

"That would be so nice! I haven't been there either," Aunty Ku'u said, "and La'i would love to step into a castle while she's here in France."

We packed a picnic lunch and waited outside. A silver station wagon pulled up and Aunty Becca jumped out to hug us while Uncle Scott got the bags. There was lots of talking and catching up as we drove through the green and yellow countryside. I stared at the bright yellow sunflowers, the rows and rows of corn, and I saw apples growing in trees for the first time!

We turned a corner and headed down a long cool pathway lined with rows of trees that looked like floating green umbrellas. In the distance we saw the huge Cinderella Castle Vaux-le-Vicomte waiting for us.

"Are you ready, La'i?" asked Aunty Becca as we stood outside the door. "Ready!" I said. We opened the door and were met by the butler of the castle, who asked if the *mademoiselle* would like to change into a gown for her visit.

"A gown?" I exclaimed. "Really?"

"Yes," Aunty Ku'u nodded to the butler, then turned to me. "La'i, choose your favorite color." I chose a pretty satin lavender gown with lace and beads and a big full skirt. Other children dressed up, too. The more daring boys put on clothes like musketeers and wore hats with big feathers on them. When I looked in the mirror, I was beautiful. A princess for a day!

As we entered the grand ballroom with its chandeliers and red velvet chairs, I heard music playing, as if asking me to dance. I looked over at Aunty Ku'u who was watching me. She smiled and nodded her permission. I picked up my skirt and as if in a dream, started to waltz across the ballroom, just like Cinderella. Some of the other girls followed me and together we laughed as we spun around in our gowns. Aunty Becca was right there clapping and taking pictures. Later, when I looked up, I spotted Aunty Kuʻu's wave which meant "OK, enough dancing," and we were off, this time to see the palace dining rooms, set for a party, with many fancy dishes and glasses.

Leaving the dining room, we entered a little Princess *chambre*, bedroom, and I stopped breathing. Everything was my size! There was a small canopy bed and a dressing table and chair. I wished I could step past the velvet rope across the room and sit down for a while. My favorite was the small velvet chair in front of the fireplace with a doll crib beside it. When I looked up, there were angels painted in the ceiling. I could have stayed there all day! It was like living inside a fairy tale.

We visited the whole castle and took pictures of everything so we would never forget.

After returning the gown to the maid, we went outside where Uncle Scott had reserved a real golf cart to travel through the huge gardens and choose a place to picnic. When we came to a shallow stream, Uncle Scott shouted "Feet up!" and drove right through it. We lifted our feet and squealed "Whee!" as we splashed along to the other side.

We laid out our picnic in a shady spot. Everything was delicious, especially the "heart cheese" with the crusty French bread, chicken and cold fruit.

Chapter 7

EXPLORING THE CITY

On one of the other days, Aunty Ku'u and I took the Metro to the Louvre Museum to see the Leonardo Da Vinci paintings and the Egyptian Exposition. Taking the metro was like riding through underground caves with lots of people who are in a hurry. It took us right to the Louvre! We rode the escalator up to the street and the fresh air, and there was the famous glass pyramid looking like a gigantic star that had fallen from the sky. We went in and found the Mona Lisa. I wondered why there were so many people staring at her. As we left, I whispered to Aunty, "I'm sure she was smiling at me!"

We hurried over to the Egyptian Exposition to see the once buried treasures of the kings and queens, just like the ones in our history books. It was awesome! As I looked around at everything I thought, *I feel so lucky. I wish my sisters were here.*

We were hungry by the time we came out, so Aunty said, "Let's try a *crêpe*," a French pancake treat. We went up the street and came to a little stand with people waiting in line. Finally, when it was our turn, we ordered *jambon et fromage*, a ham and cheese crêpe. The edges were crispy and lacy and it tasted so 'ono with the warm cheese and ham wrapped up in a cone. The first bite was yummy!

With our crêpes in hand, we took a trip on a red double-decker bus to see the city. The wind blew in our faces and the sun was hot as we bumped along.

When Aunty checked the time, she shouted "Time to go!" We both jumped off the bus at the next stop and headed to hula practice where Leilani was waiting for us.

After practice, Aunty Kuʻu and the advanced hula sisters showed us how to make our lei and *kūpeʻe*, wristlets and anklets, for our performance. Everybody helped each other and the older girls were patient with us and didn't get upset when our kūpeʻe started to go crooked. We worked carefully with the ferns that we brought from Hawaiʻi. They were precious to us because they were from our homeland and important for our hula. After we made the kūpeʻe, we bagged them and placed them in the refrigerator to stay cool.

"Can you believe we're dancing tomorrow?" I asked.

"And tomorrow," one of the girls said, " is also a big day for France, July 14th, Bastille Day!"

"What is Bastille Day?" I asked. The girls each spoke excitedly to tell the story of how for years cruel rulers kept many prisoners in the Bastille prison, and it was on July 14, 1789 that they were finally freed by courageous men.

"To this day, we celebrate with all kinds of parties, concerts, and fireworks."

I told them about our Independence Day on the 4th of July, a day when we celebrate our freedom to be American and the beginning of our own country. We celebrate with parties and fireworks, too!

"Just think," I said, "both countries celebrating Freedom in July!"

After our kūpeʻe were done, we watched the big ladies rehearse. We loved watching them and wanted to be like them when we grew up. Aunty Kuʻu was sitting next to me and whispered, "Do you see that, La'i? They smile with their heart. Even if they're French, it shows that they understand the story of their hula. *Maika'i*. That's so good."

That night when we got home, Aunty Ku'u helped me shampoo my hair. She combed it through then put it into lots of long braids. She looped them up so the next day when she brushed it out, my hair would be full and in little waves. My costume was pressed and hanging on the door. As we lay down, I told Aunty that my head felt bumpy with the braids, like sleeping on a cabbage.

Chapter 8

KUPEʻE ANGELS

The next morning, the house was busy. We ate a quick breakfast and helped pack the car. There were lists to check: lei, instruments, costumes, mats, makeup, and water.

The famous Tuileries Gardens was the site of many cultural festivals, and we had been chosen to give a Hawaiian concert. Our hālau was waiting for us when we arrived. The big people helped unload and set up. I found my hula sisters and we put our own things away. All of us had braids to undo, and Aunty Kuʻu helped us.

All of a sudden we noticed Aunty Kilohana put her hands up to her cheeks with a big worried look. She started looking everywhere and everybody started helping. Aunty Kuʻulei told us to stay with the other dancers as she hurried to her side.

"What's wrong?" she asked quietly.

"The kūpeʻe," Aunty said. "We can't find the kūpeʻe. All the kūpeʻe for everyone was in a big bag, a black one." She quickly looked at her watch. "There's no time to go home. The show starts in twenty minutes."

"Oh well," she said, "We'll just go on without it. Let's not worry. There's nothing we can do about it now."

We were sad because our kūpeʻe made our costumes complete but there was nothing we could do.

Aunty Kilohana gathered the hālau to explain about the kūpeʻe and go over important things to remember. Aunty encouraged all of us to relax and even without our kūpeʻe we would *hoʻomau*, continue, and be fine. She wanted us to know that today was the day to demonstrate all that we had been working for, and to put everything else out of our minds. At the end, she motioned us to hold hands as she gave pule. She asked *Akua*, God, to bless all our efforts and receive our offering of aloha. After the prayer, with a smile, she kissed each of us on both cheeks. She asked us to take our places and be ready for our cues. She finished dressing and went on stage.

Just then, we noticed two people running toward the back of the dressing room with a big black bag. It was Uncle Scott and Aunty Becca carrying the kūpeʻe! Everybody gathered around them and quickly passed out the treasures of hand-woven fern.

Aunty Becca and Uncle Scott explained they had stopped by the house to get directions and had just missed us. They found the kūpeʻe bag sitting in the driveway. One of the neighbors knew exactly where we were and, *voilà*! They arrived and saved the day!

At the blowing of the *pū*, conch shell, we began. The crowd quieted and Aunty Kilohana began the Oli Aloha. The men were ready in the wings to perform Uncle Pono's *"Ka I Ka Hoe,"* the Migration Chant. We watched from a little space on the side and felt so excited! We looked like little princesses with our flowing hair, some dark and some blonde, our lei and kūpeʻe in place, each of us ready to dance for Queen Liliʻuokalani, Hawaiʻi's last monarch.

When our cue was given, we went out on stage. Aunty Kilohana's eyes were so big when she noticed our kūpeʻe! She gave us a big smile and enjoyed the surprise. It was time for us to dance!

When we finished, the audience clapped for us, and it felt so good! We walked backstage, relieved that our part was done. We watched the rest of the show from the wings and loved the music. When it was all over, we were called back for a final bow, and the clapping grew louder. It was so nice to see all the dancers smiling and happy, knowing that the audience had enjoyed the performance. What a wonderful feeling!

Chapter 9

CELEBRATE

In the dressing room, Aunty Kilohana thanked all of us for our great effort and hard work. She had by then found out about the mysterious "Kūpe'e Angels" and had them by her side to thank them personally. She also announced that she had a surprise for all of us, including the Angels. Our hālau had been chosen to perform on *le bateau l'Étoile du Soir*, The Evening Star riverboat, tonight!

"We'll have dinner and see the great fireworks for the Bastille Celebration at the Eiffel Tower! We are so fortunate to be chosen to do this. People come from all over the world to celebrate with us in France!" *Ooh, la la*! How great is that!

We arranged to meet at *Pont Alexandre III*, the bridge where the bateau was waiting for us. The long white boat had three decks, many windows, and seats for a big crowd. There was even a stage with lights. The attendants guided us to the area where our dinner was going to be served. The tables were set with white tablecloths and fancy dishes and glasses. We felt very special.

Through the windows, we could see people coming on board and taking their seats. Soon we would be sailing down the Seine and under the bridges. The weather was cool and even the moon was out to celebrate and watch the fireworks! As we began to move, the horn blew, telling the other boats we were coming. Music played, and people were even dancing. We were all up on the top deck with our hālau. My hula sisters and I giggled and hung onto the railing. Some of them had ridden the bateau before and were excited to share this experience with me, and Aunty Kuʻulei. Even Uncle Scott and Aunty Becca were excited to be a part of the big celebration.

There were crowds of people everywhere along the Seine. They were in big and little clusters having evening picnics, or in big groups watching bands playing music. Sometimes, there were people with their dogs, and sometimes people sitting alone, watching the boats go by. There were many boats on the Seine, all out to celebrate Bastille Day. As the boats passed each other, they blew their horns and we all waved. We could hear music all around. Once again, I couldn't believe I was there. Aunty Kuʻu was next to me and without saying a word she hugged me close and kissed me three times on the head!

It was show time! After a short review and pule, we dressed and took our places. Once again the pū was blown and the chanting began. Everyone's attention turned to the stage as we created for our visitors a Hawaiian experience of song and dance. We told stories of our island home with our hula, and welcomed them to come and visit. Once again we told of Queen Liliʻuokalani, her grace, kindness, and strength.

Before we knew it, our show was ending. We were all dancing "…Where we live, there are rainbows." The audience clapped and shouted, "*Encore! Encore!*" which is French for *hana hou*, do it again! We came out for our final bow and walked into the audience to greet them. "*Aloha, Bonsoir, Aloha,*" we called.

At dinner, the captain came over to thank us and say "*Bon Appétit.*" There was a French feast of tiny little *hors d'oeuvres*, appetizers, colorful and tasty salads, crusty French bread and cheese, and roasted *poulet*, chicken, with vegetables.

And then, dessert was served. The lights dimmed and in marched the waiters carrying trays of French custard lit with sparklers! Everybody clapped.

"*Crème Brûlée* for everyone," cried the captain. *Oooooh, Ooooh, la la!*

Chapter 10

SHOOTING STARS

We were talking and laughing about the great day we were having when the captain announced we were slowing down to see the fireworks. We looked toward shore. The Eiffel Tower was a mountain of dazzling lights.

We grabbed each other's hand and got back up to the top deck to wait. We could see crowds of people along the Seine gathered to do the same. No matter where you were, you had a great view. Then, with *La Marseillaise*, the French National Anthem, playing, the firework displays hit the sky in hundreds of colorful sprays bursting before our eyes. They disappeared only to return as bigger and brighter shooting stars.

The show went on and on, and each burst took my breath away. My hula sisters and I hugged each other and jumped up and down. I looked for Aunty Ku'u. I needed to be with her. I saw her talking to Aunty Kilohana. I ran over and she came to get me. Together we stood quietly in the music and thunderous noise holding on to each other. She bent down and whispered to me saying, "Take it all in, La'i. This is a memory for a lifetime. We are in Paris!"

"Thank you, Aunty," I whispered through tears, "thank you for bringing me, thank you for choosing me. I wish our whole family could be here and see this."

"Well," Aunty smiled and put her arm around me. "This moment is ours! I Choose You!" and we both laughed, saying together, "BECAUSE, you the *pretty* one just like Aunty!"

We had long hugs and said goodbye to everyone, including Uncle Scott and Aunty Becca. It was time for all of us to go home. We had many bags to carry, including the fern kūpeʻe, which we would take back to Hawaiʻi to return to the land. I learned that it was our way of saying *mahalo*, thank you. By returning these ferns to Hawaiʻi, more ferns would grow.

We were all so tired when we returned home that we dragged ourselves through the door. We exchanged hugs and turned in to our rooms for hot baths.

When I closed my eyes, I saw fireworks!

Chapter 11

FILLED WITH ALOHA

We had two days before we headed home, just enough time to shop for little gifts for the 'ohana and to pack our bags. The night before leaving, the aunties finalized plans to come to Hawai'i, and exchanged all kinds of information. Then we said our *mahalo pule*, thank you prayer, with Aunty Kilohana, Leilani, and Lala. The room was filled with aloha.

Later, as we climbed into bed, I could smell Aunty Ku'u's sweet lavender bath powder. We lay there talking about how memories are made, and how we each have the power to dream big and create joyous moments in our lives.

Aunty said, "My Tūtū always told me if you have a dream, something you really want in life, write it down in a special place, look at it often, and do something, every day, if possible, to make it happen. It will come. *Hoʻo manawa nui*, be patient, it will come."

"Aunty," I said, "when I found out I would be going to France, I was happy just because I was going to be with you, and because it was my turn. I knew we would do fun things, but I had no idea about all the wonderful memories we would make. I would love to come back to Paris someday."

Aunty reached over and smoothed back my hair. "That is a good dream, Laʻi. It gives you something to reach for. When Aunty holds you close and says 'I choose you,' whether I'm referring to you or your sisters, or anyone in our ʻohana, I'm really saying, 'Come, let's do something special together.' Because Aunty does not have children, I treasure this time with all of you, and I am so happy Mommy and Daddy let me share my life with you. It would be very empty and alone."

I took her hands and gently touched the tiny lines there. Listening to Aunty, I learned something more about her; how special she was to our 'ohana, and to me. My heart was glad. I could feel her aloha. We fell asleep listening to the rain outside, a soft kilihune rain.

Chapter 12

MEMORIES LAST FOREVER

We left Paris as the sun was setting in the golden sky. The city glowed as lights began to twinkle on, one by one. It felt as if the city were saying, "*Au revoir, La'i. À bientôt!*" Goodbye, La'i. Until later!

As we slipped into the clouds, Aunty Ku'u handed me a little package. "You may open it now," she said. I sat up to see it better. I smiled. It was a little red and gold notebook with lined pages. I looked over at her, and she asked, "What could you keep in there?"

I opened it slowly, remembering our special time last night.

"Maybe dreams could go in here," I said. "My dreams, just like Tūtū said. A place to write them down and look at them." I turned to Aunty.

"Can I write about Paris in here since it was my first dream come true?"

"You can do anything you want, La'i," Aunty smiled and gave me a hug. "Dream big, choose carefully. Life is waiting!"

HAWAIIAN GUIDE TO PRONUNCIATION

La'i	*LAH-ee*
Ku'ulei	*Koo-oo-LAY*
poi	*poy*
poke	*PO-kay*
limu kohu	*LEE-moo KO-hoo*
'inamona	*ee-nah-MO-nah*
manapua	*mah-nah-POO-ah*
Kanani	*Kah-nah nee*
Kalamau	*Kah-lah-MAH-oo*
Pikake	*Pee-KAH-kay*
Bebe	*Beh-beh*
Kilohana	*Kee-lo-HAH-na*
hālau	*hah-LAH-oo*
La'ikealoha	*Lah-EE-kay ah-LO hah*
pule	*POO-lay*
'ohana	*o-HAH-nah*
mahalo nui	*mah-HAH-lo NOO-ee*
ipu heke	*EE-poo HEH-keh*
kala'au	*kah-lah-AH-oo*

HAWAIIAN GUIDE TO PRONUNCIATION

pa'u ——————————————————*PAH-oo*

makaukau ——————————*mah-KAH-oo-KAH-oo*

Ae ————————————————————*Aye*

Oli Aloha ——————————*O-lee ah-LO-hah*

Lili'u e ——————————————*LEE-lee-oo ay*

kupe'e ————————————————*koo-PEH-eh*

maika'i ————————————————*my-KAH-ee*

ho'omau ——————————————*ho-o-MAH-oo*

Ka i ka Hoe ——————————*Kah ee kah HO-eh*

'ono ——————————————————*O-no*

Ho'o manawa nui ———*Ho-o mah-nah-wah-noo-ee*

~

FRENCH GUIDE TO PRONUNCIATION

et	*ay*
petite fleur	*peh-tee FLER*
baguette	*bah-GET*
chocolat	*show-ko-LAH*
chaud	*sho*
bonjour	*bon-JOOR*
ma chérie	*ma sher-EE*
croissant	*kwah-SAHNT*
Siene	*Sehn*
ma coeur	*ma KUR*
l'Arc de Triomphe	*lark deh tree-OMF*
Champs Elysées	*shons-ay-lee-SAY*
je vous en prie	*jeh voo sahn pree*
bonne nuit mes chéries	*bonwee mey sher-EE*
comment ça va?	*Ko-mo sah vah?*
ça va	*Sah VAH*
bien, merci	*bee-YEHN, mehr-SEE*
pain au chocolat	*pahn-o-sho-Ko-LAh*

FRENCH GUIDE TO PRONUNCIATION

pain au raison ——————————*pahn o ray-ZON*

Cathedral de ——————————*Kah-THEE-dral de*

Notre Dame ——————————*no-treh DOM*

bateaux mouches ——————————*bah-toe MOOSH*

Vaux le Vicomt ——————————*Vo leh vee-KOHMt*

mademoiselle ——————————*mah-dah-mwah-ZELL*

chambre ——————————*SHAHM-breh*

crêpe ——————————*krehp*

jambon et fromage ——————*jahm-BONE ey fho-MA-hj*

l'etoile du Soir ——————————*lay-TWAHL du swah*

bonsoir ——————————*bone-SWAH*

bon appétit ——————————*bone ah-peh-TEE*

hors d'oeuvres ——————————*or-DERVS*

crème brûlée ——————————*krehm bru-LAY*

La Marseillaise ——————————*lah mar-say-YAYS*

au revoir, abientôt ——*O ru-VWAH, Ah-bee-EN-toe*

ma chère ——————————*MA-sher*

~

ACKNOWLEDGEMENTS

Mahalo nui to Sylvie Alvarez, my favorite French tutor while we lived in France, for her patience and encouragement; to Rebecca and Scott Brubaker, whose friendship and zest for life is precious to me. Mahalo also to my daughter, Amber Kamailelaulʻi, for her kind listening, counsel, and sensitivity allowing me to tell the story that was in my heart; and lastly, for my husband Harry, for his unmatched love.